Amelia Bedelia's

•First Day of School•

Hop on the bus, Amelia Bedelia!

SCHOOL BUS

By Herman Parish

Pictures by Lynne Avril

Greenwillow Books

An Imprint of HarperCollinsPublishers

For Susan & Virginia,
there at the beginning—H. P.

For Ellie's first day of school
Love, Grandmalynnie—L. A.

Amelia Bedelia's First Day of School. Text copyright © 2009 by Herman S. Parish III.
Illustrations copyright © 2009 by Lynne Avril. First published in 2009 in hardcover;
first paper-over-board edition, 2011. All rights reserved. Manufactured in the United States of America.
For information address HarperCollins Children's Books, a division of HarperCollins Publishers,
10 East 53rd Street, New York, NY 10022. www.harpercollinschildrens.com
Gouache and black pencil were used to prepare the full-color art. The text type is Cantoria MT.
Amelia Bedelia is a registered trademark of Peppermint Partners, LLC.
Library of Congress Cataloging-in-Publication Data: Parish, Herman.
Amelia Bedelia's first day of school / by Herman Parish ; pictures by Lynne Avril. p. cm. "Greenwillow Books."
Summary: A literal-minded little girl's first day of school is filled with confusing adventures, much to her delight.
ISBN 978-0-06-154455-2 (trade bdg.) — ISBN 978-0-06-154456-9 (lib. bdg.) — ISBN 978-0-06-203274-4 (pob)
[1. First day of school—Fiction. 2. Schools—Fiction. 3. Humorous stories.] I. Avril, Lynne, (date), ill. II. Title.
PZ7.P2185Ari 2009   [E]—dc22   2008037455

14 15 16 LP 10 9 8

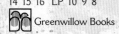 Greenwillow Books

Amelia Bedelia couldn't wait to go to school.
"Here we are," said Mrs. Park, the bus driver. "Time to jump off!"
Amelia Bedelia backed up, then ran as fast as she could,
and jumped as far as she could . . .

Amelia Bedelia landed right on top of a grown-up.

Oooooof!

"Are you my teacher?" she asked.

"I am Mrs. O'Malley. I teach gym."

"Oh," said Amelia Bedelia. "I am not Jim. I'm Amelia Bedelia.
 Can you help me find my teacher?"

"Follow me," said Mrs. O'Malley.

And Amelia Bedelia did . . . right into her new classroom.

"Hello there! My name is Miss Edwards.
 You must be Amelia."
"How did you know?" asked Amelia Bedelia.
"Because you're my last tag," Miss Edwards said.

Amelia Bedelia started running.

"You can't catch me," she yelled. "I'm too fast!"

"Come back!" said Miss Edwards, laughing.

"We aren't playing tag. I have a name tag for you."

Amelia Bedelia looked at her name tag.
Something was missing. She added "Bedelia."
"I like my whole name," she said. "It rhymes."
"So it does," said Miss Edwards. "Now please sit
wherever you like."

That was a hard choice for Amelia Bedelia.

She liked the pictures of faraway places.

She liked the letters marching across the top of the board.

She liked the hamster running on its wheel.

She liked everything she saw. So she sat down right in the middle of the classroom.

Miss Edwards began the day by calling the roll.
"Amelia Bedelia?"

"What?" said Amelia Bedelia.
"Not what," said Miss Edwards. "Here."
"I hear you," said Amelia Bedelia.
"Good," said Miss Edwards. "When you hear
  your name, say it."

"It!" hollered Amelia Bedelia.

"It?" said Miss Edwards. "Who is it?"

"I will be it!" said Amelia Bedelia. "Can we play tag now?"

Everyone began to laugh.

Clap! Clap! Clap!

"*Shhhh*. Be as quiet as mice," said Miss Edwards.
"Now that I am sure *you* are here, Amelia Bedelia,
I'll read the names of your classmates."

"Rose?"
"Here!"

Their names were very exciting, but Amelia Bedelia still loved her name best of all.

Plop! Plop! Plop!

Miss Edwards placed a lump of squishy clay on each desk.
"Let's make our favorite animals," she said.

Amelia Bedelia loved hamsters, so she began making one.

Rose made a giraffe.

Dawn made a pony.

And Clay made a big, fat bullfrog.

"You're funny, Amelia Bedelia," said Clay.
"You could be the teacher's pet."
Amelia Bedelia was not happy. She loved animals,
but she did not want to be anyone's pet.
She felt like flattening Clay's frog.

"If you have trouble, chickadees," said Miss Edwards,
"try wiggling your fingers on that clay!"

So that is exactly what Amelia Bedelia did.
Soon Clay was laughing so hard he could not stop.
"Amelia Bedelia!" said Clay. "Stop tickling me!"

"Clean up, clean up, everybody clean up!" sang
Miss Edwards. "It's time for music."
Mrs. Melody arrived with her guitar and tambourine.
"We will sing like birds today, *la-la!*" she trilled.

Tweet-tweet, chirp-chirp

Then the students toured
the library with Mr. Stacks.
"I want to see your little noses
in the books!" said Mr. Stacks.

OWW!

meow!

In gym class, Mrs. O'Malley
taught them how to run like
cheetahs.

At last it was time for lunch.

"Do you feel like a sloppy Joe?" asked the lady
behind the lunch counter.

"No!" said Amelia Bedelia. "Do I look like one?"

"Here you are," said the lady. "I hope
your eyes aren't bigger than your stomach."

"Me too," said Amelia Bedelia. "They
would not fit in my head."

"Amelia Bedelia," said Rose after
lunch. "Do you want to jump rope with us?"
Amelia Bedelia smiled. "Sure!" she said.
She put the rope on the ground and jumped over it.

Amelia Bedelia was a terrific rope jumper.
Rose giggled. So did Holly and Dawn and Joy.
But before long, everyone on the playground
was jumping rope the Amelia Bedelia way!

There was time for one last project. Miss Edwards brought
out big sheets of paper, glue, and scissors.
"This is free time," she said. "Create something wonderful!"

Amelia Bedelia decided to make daisies for her mother.

She got a piece of white paper for the petals.

And a piece of yellow paper for the centers.

And another piece of white paper.

And another piece of yellow paper.

And another piece of white paper.

And another piece of yellow paper.

"Amelia Bedelia," said Miss Edwards. "Don't be a
  Ping-Pong ball. Please sit down."
"But . . . but . . . I need green for the stems!"
"Enough is enough," said Miss Edwards. "Please glue
  yourself to your seat."

So Amelia Bedelia did. And since her daisies
didn't have stems, she glued them to her headband
until the school day ended.

"Good-bye, squirrels and ladybugs!" said Miss Edwards.
She was standing in the doorway,
giving everyone a gold star.
"See you tomorrow!"
Soon, Amelia Bedelia was the only one left.

"Amelia Bedelia," said Miss Edwards, "why are you still here?"
"Because," said Amelia Bedelia, "you told me to glue myself
 to my seat."
"So I did," said Miss Edwards.
"And so I did," said Amelia Bedelia.

Amelia Bedelia stood up, and the chair stood up with her!
Miss Edwards chuckled, then laughed out loud.
"Oh, Amelia Bedelia," Miss Edwards said. "I should have
known better than to say that to you, especially on
your first day of school."

As Miss Edwards got Amelia Bedelia unstuck,
she whispered, "Want to know a secret?
Today is my first day of school, too.
I am a brand-new teacher."
"We both deserve gold stars,"
said Amelia Bedelia.

"You'll have lots of fun tomorrow,"
said Miss Edwards. "We are
having an assembly."
"Hooray!" said Amelia Bedelia.
"What are we going to build?"

"Memories," said Miss Edwards.
Then she tapped Amelia Bedelia once,
on the very top of her head.
"Tag!" said Miss Edwards. "You are IT until tomorrow."

Amelia Bedelia smiled.
She couldn't wait to come back to school!